I KNOW I'M NOT supposed to touch niggers but Mrs. Graham's fingernails are teal and Mom's fingernails were teal the day we buried her and I touched them a lot that day. Her hands were real cold and steady. It was nice. Dad said he thought it was nice too.

Dad is waving at me now. He doesn't like me standing by the dead body. He never has. Mr. Xavier is by Dad and he starts waving at me too. I don't know Mr. Xavier that well but I like his name because not many words that start with X sound like a Z. He's nice to me though and when I walk over to them, Mr. Xavier pats my head like I'm a dog and says, Hey Lukewarm. Then he says something to Dad about putting too much of a big word I don't know how to spell and another big word I don't know how to spell in Mrs. Graham and laughs. Mrs. Graham does look more swollen than dead bodies usually do. Dad doesn't say anything but he laughs and pulls his small silver bottle from his suit and takes his 31st sip of the day.

Since Mom died Dad takes more sips. Before she died he would take nine or ten sips and he would be really silly. He'd lift Mom up and twirl her in the living room and he'd tell me knock-knock jokes. Knock knock. Who's there? Mustache. Mustache who? I mustache you a question, but I'll shave it for later. That was his favorite. I'd laugh and he'd laugh and Mom would laugh. He let me take a sip once when we were driving home from Grandma and Grandpa's. I didn't like it because it burned my throat and it made me dizzy for just a second. I told Dad I didn't like whatever was inside and I asked him why he did. He said it was because it made him calm when everything was busy. But Dad says Mr. Xavier and him are always busy because people don't stop dying, which is true. Which might be why he takes at least thirty sips a day now and isn't very silly anymore.

Dad has been really busy since Mr. Xavier called Dad and told him they were going to start putting those big words I don't know how to spell into niggers. I thought it would make Dad angry because since Mom died he's been telling people that niggers took her nerves. But Dad just shook his head, shrugged his shoulders and told Mr. Xavier, We'll just charge the coons more then.

I don't know how much Mom cost but the wake was nice and I remember people I didn't even know telling Dad,

I'm so sorry for your loss, and Dad saying back that we'll miss her more every day, which still confuses me. Am I going to miss her even more than I already do? Does thinking about her hands shaking count as missing her? Am I supposed to be keeping track of how many times I think of her every day? Miss Cawl saw that I wrote those questions on my sheet of paper one day when I was supposed to be writing something else. I was scared about what she might say but she said those were good questions to ask. Then she told me to put the questions away and start on my work. I like Miss Cawl.

Just then dad and Mr. Xavier stand up straighter because Mr. Graham walks to the front of the room and asks everyone to be seated. The room quiets down and sits. Dad takes his 32nd sip. Mr. Graham tries to talk but he doesn't get very far before he starts crying. They look like really heavy tears. I think his kids are up front because the oldest girl stands by Mr. Graham and says, We all loved my mom in some way or another and while it's a shame she's gone we know God has a plan for all of us. I raise my hand so I can ask her what God's plan is for me and if God has talked to Mom but Dad puts my arm down. He tells me to be quiet and to listen.

I'm eating by myself in the lunch room. People usually don't sit by me and that's okay. Being alone lets me think of things I wouldn't think of if I had people talking to me all the time. I keep thinking of the writing assignment Miss Cawl had us do this morning. I can picture the paper. I can remember word-for-word what I wrote.

Lucas Carlson
14 May 1962

Mother's Day

Mother's Day is Sunday, but Mom won't be there, because Mom died 113 days ago. Mom was very nice to me, and was a good mom. When I had a bad day at school, she would tickle my armpits until we both started laughing. I miss that.

She was a good cook. I really liked when she made Hot Dogs, because they would be crunchy and soft at the same time. Dad just gives them to me cold. Sometimes he tries to make things Mom used to make, but they aren't as good. I tell him it's good, but he knows it isn't so he doesn't eat much anymore.

I miss walking home from school, because Mom would meet me at Doc's General Store and walk with me the rest of the way and ask me how my day went. Now I go to Grandma and Grandpa's house most days after school, and it's not as fun, but I love them because they're Grandma and Grandpa.

I miss skipping stones with Mom at the creek, because when we would come home Dad would laugh at how wet our pants and shoes were. Dad even came once or twice, and he would skip them the farthest, and he would skip them up the creek instead of across and let the current catch the stone and make it stop. I think he might want to just stop again because he's always so busy.

Dad doesn't say he misses Mom, but I know he does because

That's when time was up so I hurried to put the commas where they were supposed to go. I really do miss skipping stones though. It was usually just me and Mom and she'd say, You're so good at it Lukie! and it would make me smile. She wasn't very good at it because of her hands but she'd always tell me how I good I was at using my eyes and to just keep those eyes up. And we would stop for ice cream at LaBelle's on the way home, even in January. But that was the month she died so I don't think I'll get ice cream in January anymore.

I take a bite of my sandwich and look around the lunch room. Gerry Langford is in line behind Josie Meekourt. Josie's the prettiest girl in school and she smells like dandelions. I think Gerry is too busy shoving kids to like dandelions. Gerry shoves the same boys around every day until a grown up gets angry and yells. Then he stops and everyone seems fine. It makes me think I have to get angry for someone to listen. But I'm not good at being angry. Maybe I'm good at being sad because it makes me sad that since Mom died Gerry doesn't push me around like he pushes the other boys.

After lunch, I go to class. And after school, I go to Grandma and Grandpa's. When I get there, Grandma asks if I think we can finish the puzzle we've been working on for 34 days. I tell her, I don't think so but we can try, and she smiles and puts a piece in the bottom right corner, which completes a building next to the church that takes up most of the puzzle. Grandma says the church is in New York City and that she's been there once and that it's one of the prettiest things she has ever seen. She says, If God isn't in that church I have no idea where he is. I ask her if she thinks that's where God does all of his planning and she laughs and says, Maybe.

Grandpa walks into the kitchen and asks how I'm doing. Grandpa's a lot bigger than Grandma in every way but his voice is just as high, which seems strange to me because Dad and Mr. Xavier have really deep voices. I tell him, I'm good, and he says, Good, and gets himself some potato chips and walks out of the kitchen. After Mom died Grandpa wouldn't come out of the bedroom and see me when I came over. I've never asked why but I think it's because Grandpa told me once that I look a lot like Audrey and he didn't want to see her anymore. Mom did say that her and Grandpa didn't always see things the same way.

###

Dad picks me up around 6:00. The car smells stale and sour at the same time and I ask Dad, What's making that smell? He says, I don't smell anything, but I still do so I roll down my window. Dad says, I'll show you where it smells bad, and rolls his window down to smoke. I don't like the smell of smoke either so I put my nose close to my window.

We drive the opposite direction of home and outside there are some white kids playing. Girls in dresses chase one another around a yard while boys that are a few years older than me throw a baseball back and forth. Dad says this is a good neighborhood. I agree because I see dads sitting on their decks and drinking and moms sitting in their yards trying to catch the sun, which is something Mom used to say.

As Dad passes Jackson's Pharmacy, he says that this is where it gets bad, but I don't know what he means. It's quiet like the other one and kids are playing in yards like the other one and in parks. Next to Jackson's is Fred's, which is a restaurant I've never been to. It smells really good. It smells like the food stand at the fair. I ask Dad why he thinks this is such a bad neighborhood and he says, It's too dark here. I tell him, The sun is still out. He says, The sun can't make niggers any lighter. We drive past Fred's and I see a nigger boy about my size and with hair as orange as mine being pushed around by two boys bigger than Gerry Langford. It really doesn't seem that bad to me.

###

I guess Dad and I aren't going to church. I woke up at 7:30 because Mom always woke up at 7:30 on Sundays. I waited until 8:00 to wake Dad up but when I tried he started talking in his sleep and I couldn't understand what he said. The room smelled like Dad spilled at least 22 sips on his sheets.

I think about going to church by myself but I don't think Dad would be happy to wake up and see me gone. I don't think he'll be happy when he wakes up and church is over either. I'm confused about what I should do. So I go back to my room and get dressed. I don't know how to tie ties so I wait for Dad to wake up because it won't take him very long to tie my tie for me. He doesn't wake up until 9:45 though and when he does I'm sitting on the stairs. He walks past me and says, Good morning Lukewarm, and I say it back but I don't think it's a good morning because we missed church and I wonder if God will have a new plan for both of us now. I say, We missed church, and Dad just nods.

The phone rings. Dad answers it and I listen from the stairs. Dad says that he's sorry and then takes a long pause and says that he knows everybody's wondering about him and me and more so now that we didn't go to church and he says he's sorry again but it doesn't sound like he means it and he says, Goodbye, and hangs up. I go into the kitchen and ask, Who was that? Dad cracks some eggs and says it was Grandma.

The phone rings again while we're eating. Dad sighs and tells me to answer it. Mr. Xavier is on the other end and says, Hey Lukewarm, and asks for Dad. I tell Dad it's Mr. Xavier. Dad shakes his head then picks up the phone and says, Yeah? I walk back to the dining room and hear Dad say, Another nigger? Then he says, Jesus Christ. Mom wouldn't like him saying that. Then I think Mr. Xavier makes a joke because Dad laughs and says, Can you handle it for now though? I wait for Dad to hang up before I ask what Mr. Xavier wanted. Dad says, Nothing, then asks how the eggs taste. I say, Good, but I don't like that I did because Mom wouldn't like me lying like that.

When Dad gets out of the shower he comes into the living room. He smells a lot better now. He sits next to me on the sofa with the Sunday paper that Johnny Winston threw at our door this morning. Dad likes to look at the sports section. He always gives me the obituaries page because he says he knows who died already. In today's obituaries are Thomas J. Ketchen, Sally Marigold Bosnick, Lois Deborah Thorpe, Orwell Thurston Podge, Brian Jefferson Waldrip, Audrey F. Trinks. I stop there for a second because I always do when I see the name Audrey. It makes me think about Mom's obituary that I cut out and put in a box I keep under my bed:

Audrey Christine Carlson
(2 September 1931 - 26 January 1962)

Audrey Christine Carlson, 30, of Ozark, went home to be with the Lord Thursday January 26, 1962. She was a loving wife, proud and devoted mother, and all one could ask for in a daughter. The family is grateful for the support they've received in this time of need.

Audrey was born Sept. 2, 1931 to Mitchell A. Rysmith and Eleanor (Denison) Rysmith. Audrey graduated from Sterling County High School in 1949, where she soon after met her husband, Walter Carlson of Tuscaloosa, AL.

Walter and Audrey were married March 21, 1951 in Ozark. Audrey worked at Nails and Such Salon as a manicurist until she became pregnant with her son, Lucas.

She is survived by her husband, Walter; her son, Lucas; her parents, Mitchell and Eleanor Rysmith; sister, Doris (Rysmith) Engles of Tallahassee, FL. She was preceded in death by her grandparents, Alfred and Betsy Rysmith, her father-in-law Reginald Milo Carlson, her mother-in-law Mildred Frances Carlson, and her brother, John, who was taken too early by disease as well.

Audrey will be remembered for being the spark of her family, for having the spirit of the Lord and for passing that on to her husband and son. She will be greatly missed by all.

The funeral service for Audrey is Sunday, January 29, 1:00 p.m. at St. Anthony's Catholic Church in Ozark with Father Charles Shea officiating. Arrangements made by Xavier Funeral Parlor.

I remember Grandma kept tissues on the table when she wrote it. Dad was quiet but kept nodding when Grandpa read what Grandma wrote. After Grandpa finished reading he looked at Dad and said, You really don't have to prepare her. Dad just asked if teal was okay. Grandma and Grandpa smiled. Then Dad left for Mr. Xavier's and Grandpa went to the bedroom.

Dad turns the radio to a baseball game and puts the sports section on the floor. He takes sips but I don't know what numbers yet. I keep looking over the obituaries because I can't find Mrs. Graham. I couldn't find her last week either. I ask Dad why I can't find Mrs. Graham and he says it's because the paper doesn't print anything about the death of a nigger. I tell him, That's mean, and he asks why and I say, Because niggers should be included, and he says, Sure. I ask Dad if he has a wake tomorrow and he says, Yes. I tell him I want to go. He asks me why and I say, Because I like Mr. Xavier's, but it's really because I want to hear the family talk about God's plan again. I want to know what it means. I would ask Dad but I don't think he'll want to talk about it, especially if he doesn't want to go to church anymore. He'd just tell me to ask Grandma or Grandpa and I don't want to do that either. I don't want Grandpa to go back to the bedroom and I don't want Grandma to cry. I hate seeing her cry.

I don't want you at any more wakes, Dad says. End of story, he says. I tell him, I'm not a baby. He says he knows and asks if I want to go play catch instead of argue. I say, Sure, and I'm excited because we haven't played catch in 242 days.

In the yard Dad waves at people driving by and honking their horns. I remember one time I asked Dad, Why do so many people know you? And I remember him saying, Because every living person knows someone who died, which makes sense. Ready Lukewarm? Dad asks now and I say, I'm ready, and he throws the ball really high so that I lose it in the sun. But I catch it. I catch it because 297 days ago I begged Dad to show me how to handle a fly ball. I toss the ball back and tell him to throw it faster. He says, OK, and he throws it faster. I catch it and he says, That's great Lukewarm, and I toss him back the ball as fast as I can. Dad misses the ball. He's breathing heavier than I've ever heard him breathe and he's sweating more than I've ever seen him sweat. He picks up the ball. I say, Throw it faster, and he throws it faster. I catch it again and it hurts my hand. I toss the ball back but Dad misses the ball again. He starts walking toward the ball but then all of a sudden he stops and takes his glove off and throws it at the house. Then he grabs the ball and throws that at the house too and it makes a huge Thwack when it hits the door. Between deep breaths he says, I'm going to sleep, and walks inside.

Grandma asks me to help her with her flowers and I say I will. Grandpa says he'll help too. As soon as we go outside

Grandma starts pulling weeds in the flower bed. For being so old she can bend over really far. Grandpa walks over to me and says, She's flexible huh? Grandma says to stop it but she laughs and he laughs and I laugh too but I don't know what I'm laughing at.

Grandpa asks Grandma where she wants all the flowers that are sitting in pots on the lawn. Grandma says she'll decide in a minute. Grandpa sits down on the grass and it looks like going from standing to sitting hurts him. He hurt his shoulder before I was born. I don't know how it happened but I can see it on his face that it still bothers him.

I sit next to him and look at the clouds. One of them looks like a cat with its tail curled and I point that out to Grandpa. Grandpa agrees and points out another one and says it looks like a whale. I don't think it looks like a whale but I don't tell him that. I ask, What kind of whale? He says, Blue, and I nod because it's the only kind of whale I've ever heard of. Neither of us talk for a few seconds but I wish I had more to say to him.

After the clouds pass over, Grandpa picks a flower from one of the pots and hands it to me. He tells me to smell it. I think it smells like Mom but I know not to tell him it smells like Audrey. I tell him I like it. He says he's always liked those flowers. He tells me they're called hy-a-cinth. I ask him why he likes them so much and he says that his mom had them around their house when he was a kid. It's hard for me to picture Grandpa as a kid. His hair now is silver so I don't know what color his hair could've been then or if his nose was any smaller. Mom always told me I had Grandpa's nose but I don't think our noses look alike at all.

I ask Grandpa if we could put some hy-a-cinth-s around Mom's grave and he says, There are already some there. Grandma tosses an orange flower on the grass and says, We can take that one to Audrey's grave. I say, What about that yellow one? Grandma gives me that one too. After we have a bunch of colors Grandpa asks me if I miss Mom and I say I do and he rubs my head and says, I miss her a lot too.

Dad pulls into the driveway. He walks real slow and his eyes are shiny but have big bags weighing them down. Dad looks at the flowers and says they look good. Grandpa says, Lukie here did most of the work, and I laugh and say, No I didn't. Dad looks at me and says, It looks good. I tell Dad we're going to take a bunch of flowers to Mom's grave. He doesn't smile or anything but he says, That's good. Then Grandpa asks Dad if he's doing OK and Dad says, I'm doing just fine.

###

We stayed inside for gym class and threw footballs to each other because it was raining. Gerry Langford was my partner but he wasn't trying very hard and threw the balls up high and soft. I caught every one of them and told him to throw the ball faster but he never did. I started dropping the balls on purpose because I thought maybe Gerry would get mad at me and push me or throw them faster. But he just kept telling me I was doing a good job. Then he made fun of Garrett Billings for dropping so many balls next to us and it had me really sad and I don't like that Gerry Langford makes me sad.

I'm not so sad when the sun comes out but it makes me think about going to the creek after school instead of Grandma and Grandpa's. Even though it's been 151 days since the last time I skipped stones, I don't think Grandpa would want to go because it would hurt his shoulder. And Grandma's not really into that kind of thing because she likes puzzles and flowers. I don't know who else to ask because the only other person that talks to me is Miss Cawl and all she says now is, Good job, when she hands me my work. But that's all. This morning she just set my Mother's Day writing on my desk and said, Lucas, and moved on to other kids after looking at me like I was supposed to say I was sorry for something.

The bell rings and Miss Cawl reminds us of the math homework for tonight that I started at lunch. I walk behind Josie Meekourt on the way out of school. Because she likes dandelions so much I thought she'd notice the yellow shirt I wore today. But she didn't. She still smells really good so I can't be mad at her. She walks to the buses in front of the school, which is the way I'm supposed to go to Grandma and Grandpa's. But I stop and let other kids walk past me. I don't want to go to Grandma and Grandpa's today. I think about going to the creek again but I know I can't do that by myself. The only place other than Grandma and Grandpa's I can go is to Mr. Xavier's.

###

I walk into Mr. Xavier's and there are niggers in black everywhere. Some are seated and some are standing but they're all looking at me. I think it's because of the yellow shirt. All the stares makes me nervous. But none of them stare for very long because there are a bunch of nigger kids younger than me running around and laughing, which is better than crying. At Mom's wake there were a lot of young kids that didn't know how to act either and their parents let them run around because they were too busy talking to Dad or Grandma and Grandpa and crying.

I wait at the front for Dad but he never comes so I walk to the casket. It's really small. When I look inside I see a nigger boy about my size and in a black suit that's too big. His skin doesn't look like it's about to burst like Mrs. Graham's did. I look closer. His hands are together over his belly and his tie is around his neck and his orange hair looks red under the light and I can see a smear from a kiss on his right cheek. His eyes are shut really tight and so are his lips. I want to touch him but I know I'm not supposed to.

After the clouds pass over, Grandpa picks a flower from one of the pots and hands it to me. He tells me to smell it. I think it smells like Mom but I know not to tell him it smells like Audrey.

Just then someone asks me who I am and I turn around to see it's a boy that looks exactly like the boy in the casket. Exactly like him! The only difference is that his eyes are open. I tell him, I'm Lucas Carlson, and he says his name is Carlton Smiths. I say my last name and his first name are almost exactly the same but he doesn't laugh or smile like I do. He tells me he's never seen me before. I say I haven't seen him either. I say, I don't see many niggers with orange hair. Carlton pushes me in the shoulder and says, Don't call me that. I say, I'm sorry, and I really am because I didn't know. I think of all the times Dad has said that word and I wonder if he knows he isn't supposed to say it. He asks if I knew his brother and I say, No I didn't. He says they were twins and I say, That's strange, because I've never seen twins before. He tells me it was nice having a twin because sometimes they would even dress alike on their aunt's birthday and would play tricks on her and their uncle and their cousins. I say, That would be funny.

Carlton tells me he feels weird that everybody is sad and I tell him that everybody is supposed to be sad. He says, Really? I say, I know because Mom died 118 days ago. Carlton asks, How did she die? I say, Her hands kept shaking and her legs quit working. Carlton says he's sorry to hear that and I say, I'm sorry about your brother. Carlton points to his brother's hands and says, He was stabbed. I say, Stabbed? Carlton says, With a knife. I don't know why anyone would want to stab Carlton's twin. I ask, Was it someone like me? Carlton says, They were white but they were older than you, and I say, Good, because if it were someone like me I would feel really bad. But then I feel bad for saying good and I say, I'm sorry. Just then an older dark woman says, Carlton! Get over here! Carlton says it was nice to meet me and I say, It was nice to meet you, and Carlton walks over to the older dark woman.

I feel a tug on my backpack. I almost fall over. It's Dad and his breath smells like he just took his 40th sip. He says, What the hell are you doing here? I don't want to make him angrier so I tell him the truth. I say, I didn't feel like going to Grandma and Grandpa's. He squats down and says, You can't be here. I ask him, Why not? He says that this is no place for a young boy alive or dead. I tell him that I've been here before and that I can behave. He says, That doesn't matter, and tells me to go to his office and to do my homework.

Dad takes me up to the office and calls Grandma and tells her that I'm at Mr. Xavier's. He sounds really frustrated and tells me to stay put. Before I can tell him I will, he slams the door shut. I do stay put for a while but there's a window up here so between math problems I walk to the window and look outside at the parking lot. Eventually all the people come outside and I spot Carlton walking to a car with the woman that called him over earlier. I try to open the window but I can't figure out the locks. So I tap on the window and hope that Carlton sees me but he doesn't. The rest of the people down there look up instead. Dad is out there too and looks up and shakes his head. I watch him walk inside and I can hear him jog up the stairs. I sit back down at the desk and act like I'm busy.

###

Miss Cawl told us to write about friends today.

Lucas Carlson

21 May 1962

My New Friend

I made a new friend yesterday. His name is Carlton. I met him at Mr. Xavier's because that's where Dad works. I met Carlton while I was looking at his twin brother who was stabbed. I never learned his dead twin's name because Dad made me go to his office. But I know they were twins because Carlton said so. I think I met Carlton because I've been looking for a friend and maybe it's God's plan that he made up in a church in New York City.

Dad wasn't happy that I went to Mr. Xavier's after school because I was supposed to go to Grandma and Grandpa's but I didn't want to. I'm glad I didn't because me and Carlton are friends now. But I don't know if Dad will like that because I think Dad will just say he's a dark boy and I can't be friends with him. I hope that's not true because Carlton was really nice.

###

I can't tell if Miss Cawl liked My New Friend or not because all the paper said when she gave it back was to see her at lunch today. She's never asked me to eat lunch with her before. So at first I was scared but now I think it's fine because eating alone today would have me thinking about too many things.

After the other kids leave the room I walk up to Miss Cawl's desk and pull the sandwich out of my backpack. I say, Miss Cawl you said you wanted to see me. She gets up from the desk and closes the door. Her perfume smells like those hy-a-cinth-s at Grandma and Grandpa's. She tells me to sit down and says, Lucas I'm worried about you. She says that my work has been alarming lately. Then Miss Cawl says that not many kids write about death. I say, Dad works with death every day. She says that she knows that and then she asks if I miss Mom a lot and I say I do, a whole lot. Then she asks if anybody else knows that I miss Mom. I say Grandma and Grandpa do. She asks if Dad does and I tell her, I think so. She says maybe her and Dad should talk. I say, OK, and that I think Dad will like her. She says, OK, and that she'll call him after school today. I say, OK, and that he really likes baseball. She says, OK, and tells me to go eat my lunch with the other kids. I don't want to but I say, OK.

###

Dad didn't say anything about Miss Cawl last night and he's still sleeping. It's already 8:30 and it's a really sunny Saturday. I think Dad could want to go to the creek today so I try to wake him up. His room smells really bad again and the small silver bottle is on the floor. I pick it up and it's almost empty. When I try to wake him up he coughs and turns onto his side. I nudge him one more time and he says, Not now.

I wait for over two hours and Dad still isn't awake. I go into his room again. His shirt is off now and his small silver bottle is on the floor and when I pick it up this time it's totally empty, which means he'll be asleep for a while longer. But I really want to go outside. I push on his back again and he says, Not now Lukewarm.

I look out the kitchen window at our yard. The grass is really long and probably needs to be cut but Dad doesn't want me cutting the yard by myself so I go into the kitchen and pour a glass of milk and drink that. I wonder if Carlton likes milk as much as I do. I wonder if Carlton likes ice cream. Maybe Carlton likes caramel in his ice cream. Maybe Carlton and his twin went to LaBelle's like Mom and me used to. Maybe Carlton would want to skip stones with me and then go to LaBelle's. He might like it because he might still be sad and he might want to talk about his dead brother and I might want to talk about my dead mom while we eat our ice cream. I could tell him about her hands and we could figure out God's plan for both of us.

I start walking toward where Dad said the dark people live. It's really quiet outside and there aren't too many cars on the road except for next to Roger's Diner, which is really busy on Saturdays. So I look both ways before I cross the road and keep walking toward Grandma and Grandpa's. I remember to walk a street behind their house because I don't want them to see me. If they see me they'll tell me to come inside or they'll call Dad to come and get me because they'll say they are worried about me, just like Miss Cawl. Sometimes it's nice having people worried about you and other times it isn't so nice.

I walk on the sidewalk behind Fred's and it smells so good here and so warm and so much like two Easters ago when Mom and Grandma cooked ham and potatoes and lamb. But through an open door I see some dark men cutting meat on the counter with big knives. I think of Carlton's twin and being stabbed and I start to walk faster. I pass dark women sitting on a picnic table taking pits out of peaches and plums. They smile at me and I smile back. Then I walk past some dark boys playing with a basketball and they are laughing and I start running to them because one of them has orange hair. When I get closer I see it isn't Carlton. I ask them if they know where Carlton's at and they run away from me, across the street, which makes me sad. It's sad that we run away from people who just want to talk.

Farther up the sidewalk there are some dark people standing outside of the movies. They're all dressed real nice and talking about something they're going to see. Any of the kids move away from me when I walk by so when I see an old man with really thick and smart grey eyebrows I ask him if he knows Carlton. His voice is really scratchy when he says he doesn't know a Carlton and I point to my hair and say, He has orange hair like this. He says, Don't know him, and I say, OK, and walk to another older man and ask him too. He says he doesn't know a Carlton.

When I walk to another old man a woman walks up to me and touches my shoulder and asks me my name. I tell her, I'm Lucas Carlson. She says her name is Loretta. I think that's a good name for her because it makes me think of a tall lady in a pink dress, which is what she is. Loretta asks me what I'm doing today and I say, I'm looking for my friend Carlton. I ask her if she knows him. She says she doesn't know a Carlton. Then she asks why I'm looking for him and I say, Because we're going to skip stones at the creek like Mom and I did 154 days ago. Loretta asks me where Mom is and I tell her Mom has been dead for 121 days. She says she's sorry to hear that. I tell her, It's OK, because Carlton's brother has been dead for three days. She tells me the next time I see Carlton to tell him that she's sorry and I say, I will. I say, Thank you Loretta, and start walking but she stops me and asks where Dad is. I tell her he's still sleeping because he drank over 40 sips from his small silver bottle. Loretta's eyes turn sad. She looks back at the group of people she was standing next to. Then she looks at me and says, Like a flask? I say, What's a flask? She shapes her hands into a square and says, They're silver and people put things that taste like fire into them. I say, That has to be it then. She shakes her head and asks where I live. I tell her, I live 14 blocks away but Grandma and Grandpa live 9 blocks away. She squats down and tells me she wants to see where Grandma and Grandpa live. I grab her hand and tell her I'll show her.

We walk past Jackson's Pharmacy and past Fred's and Loretta asks me how old I am. I tell her, I'll be eight in August. She says, August is a good month, and I say, It sure is. Then a few cars drive by and honk their horns but they don't wave like when me and Dad were playing catch. They just scream words I'm not supposed to say. Loretta looks sad for a minute but asks me what Dad does. I tell her he works at Mr. Xavier's and that he puts big words into dead people and at first all she says is, Oh. Then she asks me what I like to do and I tell her I like to skip stones and that I like wakes and she says that seems odd. I say, I like them because I want to hear more about God's plan. She says she likes that. I tell her, That's where I met Carlton. She says that it sounds like a good place to meet a friend because we all need friends at a time like that. I say, I know.

Both Grandma and Grandpa are outside on their porch and when they see me and Loretta they walk down their steps real fast and grab my hand. Grandma looks like she has been crying. Why would she be crying? Did Grandpa say something mean? Grandpa's voice is never mean. I hug Grandma and say, I don't like it when you cry. Then Loretta says, I'm Loretta, and, It's nice to meet you, and then smiles. Grandma lets go of me and smiles but she doesn't look like she means it. Grandpa asks me where I was. I say, I was looking for Carlton because I wanted to skip stones at the creek like Mom and me used to. Then Loretta says she found me by myself at the movies and that I said they lived here and so she brought me here. Grandpa says, Thank you. Loretta says, You're welcome, and I like how soft her voice sounds when she says it. I say, Thank you Loretta. She says, No problem sweetheart, and I like that she says sweetheart too. Then Loretta walks down the sidewalk alone. All I can think about is how I really want to know what Loretta thinks about when she's alone.

Grandma says, Come inside Lukie, but before we get to the door Dad pulls into the driveway. The car screeches real loud before Dad gets out. Grandpa says, He's OK Walter he's OK, but Dad says, I need to talk to him, and, We're going home. Grandpa starts saying something but Dad says, Not now Mitch, and Grandpa takes Grandma inside. Dad says, Get in the damn car now Lucas, and I do. He gets in and slams his door and starts the car and we take off and he doesn't look at me. He says, What the hell were you doing? What were you thinking? I say, I was looking for Carlton so we could go skip stones at the creek like Mom and me used to. He says, Who the hell is Carlton? I say, Carlton is my friend. I leave out the color of Carlton's skin because I don't want Dad to be any angrier, and I don't want to lie and say that he is white. Dad breathes really heavy and he says, You scared me to death Luke. I say, I didn't want to scare you to death. I really didn't. I don't want Dad to die too. He says, It's OK.

At a stop sign Dad asks me if I miss skipping stones with Mom and I say, Yes. He says, I miss her too. I say, You don't show it. He says, What do you mean? I say, You're too busy, and he doesn't say anything. Then he says, Miss Cawl called the other day to say that she's worried about you. I ask

Dad if he likes her and he says, She seems like a nice person. Then Dad asks me what I miss most about Mom. I say, Everything. Then I ask him what he misses most about her. He doesn't say anything for a few seconds but then Dad presses the gas pedal and we start moving again. Then he says, I miss her cheeks. I say, Her cheeks? He says, They were the softest things these hands have ever felt, and he laughs and I laugh and he laughs at me laughing. Then he reaches for his flask and I stop laughing.

FLASK

a *Strays Like Us* story by Garrett Francis

ABOUT THE AUTHOR

Garrett Francis is the author of the novel *And in the Dark They Are Born* and the short story collection *Strays Like Us*. He grew up on a small farm in Michigan and earned his B.A. in Creative Writing from Grand Valley State University.

In 2012, Garrett co-founded *Squalorly*, a digital literary journal of the Midwest and served as its nonfiction editor until 2014.

In 2016, founded Orson's Publishing in 2016, a micro press and served as the press's sole editor (and designer, and publicist, among other roles) until its closure in 2020, publishing four book-length works by new and emerging authors.

He also founded *Orson's Review* in 2017, a digital literary journal that served as a companion to its parent press, publishing fiction, creative nonfiction, poetry and photography. He served as the sole editor of *Orson's Review* as well, and is proud to have helped bring the work of over 70 international contributors to life.

Today, Garrett lives in the Pacific Northwest with his family. Short works of his have been published in literary journals like *Midwestern Gothic*, *Barely South Review*, *Whiskeypaper* and *Monkeybicycle*.

Visit authorgarrettfrancis.com to learn more about Garrett and his work.

This is a work of fiction in which all events and characters in this book are completely imaginary. Any resemblance to actual people is entirely coincidental.

ISBN: 978-1-7338171-6-5

Published by 5626 Press

* 9 7 8 1 7 3 3 8 1 7 1 6 5 *